Blushing Becky

A story in a
familiar setting

This edition first published in 2010 by
Sea-to-Sea Publications
Distributed by Black Rabbit Books
P.O. Box 3263, Mankato, Minnesota 56002

Text © Jillian Powell 2005, 2010
Illustration © Kate Sheppard 2005

Printed in USA

Library of Congress Cataloging-in-Publication Data

Powell, Jillian.
  Blushing Becky / written by Jillian Powell ; illustrated by Kate Sheppard.
       p. cm. -- (Reading corner)
  Summary: Becky blushes at the smallest things, and as her class prepares to put on
a play her cheeks redden over and over but when it is time to perform, she becomes
a tiger.
  ISBN 978-1-59771-233-0 (hardcover)
  [1. Blushing--Fiction. 2. Theater--Fiction. 3. Schools--Fiction.] I. Sheppard, Kate, ill.
II. Title.
  PZ7.P87755Blu 2010
  [E]--dc22
                                    2008045860

9 8 7 6 5 4 3 2

Published by arrangement with the Watts Publishing Group Ltd., London

Series Editor: Jackie Hamley
Series Advisors: Dr. Linda Gambrell, Dr. Barrie Wade, Dr. Hilary Minns
Series Designer: Peter Scoulding

Blushing Becky

Written by
Jillian Powell

Illustrated by
Kate Sheppard

SEA-TO-SEA
Mankato Collingwood London

Jillian Powell

"We all blush sometimes. It's as natural as laughter or tears. The Ancient Greeks even had a special word for 'fear of going red'!"

Kate Sheppard

"I was always blushing, just like Becky. The more I worried about it, the more I blushed. I still blush now, but I don't mind so much!"

Becky blushed at the smallest thing.

She blushed when she sat next
to the boy she liked best in class.

She blushed even more
when he smiled at her.

Now Becky had something else to blush about. Her class was putting on a play at the end of the school year.

Becky had to paint a tree. But green paint kept splashing EVERYWHERE! The more green paint she splashed, the redder she blushed.

11

The next day, it was time to learn
the words. Everyone had to stand
on stage and read out loud.

Soon it was Becky's turn.

She blushed as red as her socks.

The next week, they had to practice the music. Becky tried to play a recorder.

But it just made a horrible squeaky sound. She blushed as red as her sweater.

"Never mind, Becky," said her
teacher. "Try these cymbals instead."

"This is fun!" Becky thought.

Then CRASH! BANG! "Whoops!"

Becky blushed even more.

19

The week after, they had to learn a dance. When the teacher stopped the music, they all had to make animal statues. Becky was being a tiger.

21

Becky stopped...

...she wobbled...

...then she fell down.

And Becky blushed as red
as her hair ribbons.

Now it was time to make the
costumes. They needed animal
masks for the dance. Becky
made a fierce tiger mask.

At last, everything was ready. It was
time for everyone to come and watch.

snap snap

"Hurray!" they all cheered
and clapped when it was over.

And Becky blushed redder
than ever...

...but Tiger didn't!

Notes for parents and teachers

READING CORNER has been structured to provide maximum support for new readers. The stories may be used by adults for sharing with young children. Primarily, however, the stories are designed for newly independent readers, whether they are reading these books in bed at night, or in the reading corner at school or in the library.

Starting to read alone can be a daunting prospect. READING CORNER helps by providing visual support and repeating words and phrases, while making reading enjoyable. These books will develop confidence in the new reader, and encourage a love of reading that will last a lifetime.

If you are reading this book with a child, here are a few tips:

1. Make reading fun. Choose a time to read when you and the child are relaxed and have time to share the story.

2. Encourage children to reread the story, and to retell the story in their own words, using the illustrations to remind them what has happened.

3. Give praise. Remember that small mistakes need not always be corrected.

READING CORNER covers three grades of early reading ability, with three levels at each grade. Each level has a certain number of words per story, indicated by the number of bars on the spine of the book, to allow you to choose the right book for a young reader:

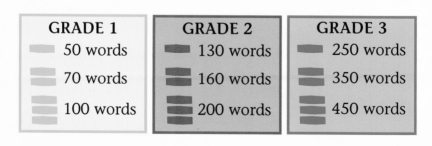

GRADE 1	GRADE 2	GRADE 3
50 words	130 words	250 words
70 words	160 words	350 words
100 words	200 words	450 words